FREEING FREDDIE
the Dream Weaver

D1441410

Other Books by Brent Feinberg

Freeing Freddie the Dream Weaver
A Guide to Realizing Your Dreams: A Workbook
with Kim Normand

Freeing Freddie the Dream Weaver
The Ultimate Activity Book
with Kim Normand

FREEING FREDDIE

the Dream Weaver

BRENT FEINBERG

ILLUSTRATED BY
DANIEL CLARKE

SQUAREONE
PUBLISHERS

ISBN 978-0-7570-0458-2 (print) / ISBN 978-0-7570-5458-7 (ebook)

Manufactured in China

10 9 8 7 6 5 4 3 2 1

"We do not believe in ourselves until someone reveals that deep inside us something is valuable, worth listening to, worthy of our trust, sacred to our touch. Once we believe in ourselves we can risk curiosity, wonder, spontaneous delight or any experience that reveals the human spirit."

e.e. Cummings

Here, in the beautiful rainforest of life, the mystical journey of Freddie begins.

Freddie was walking through the magical rainforest. He felt the lush green grass gently brushing beneath the soles of his feet. He marvelled at the sensation.

He paused walking for a few moments and took five deep breaths.

Freddie felt his lungs fill all the way. The air was fresh and sweet. Freddie's best friends were the trees. Freddie could not imagine what life would be like without all the beautiful, giant trees, which created the very air he breathed.

F reddie wandered deeper into the magical rainforest.
It opened up on to a vast meadow. Beautiful flowers of
all colors and sizes surrounded him. Big pink roses, gentle
yellow tulips and thousands of tiny white daisies.
Freddie had played and frolicked about the rainforest
and meadows his whole life. Since as far back as
Freddie could remember the rainforest was home.

One day Freddie stumbled and fell. He rolled down a hill and became entangled in a large spider web. He was trapped. He tried and tried but could not move. He was suddenly very scared. He yelled out,

"Help me, can anybody help me?"

A sound from above caught Freddie's attention. He glanced over his shoulder and saw a giant spider, slowly descending along its web from the trees above. Freddie began to tremble and shake, consumed with fear.

Paralyzed with terror, entangled in the old spider web,
Freddie lay caught, speechless as the spider came near.

"Hello," said the giant spider, *"My name is Mr. Cotton."*

Freddie was amazed at how friendly Mr. Cotton the
giant spider sounded and he began to relax.
Quietly he responded, "Hi, my name is Freddie."

Mr. Cotton said, *"Freddie, if you desire,*
I can show you how to untangle yourself
from the old spider web that you are trapped in
and create a new web, the web of your dreams."

"How can I do that?" asked Freddie.

"Anything is possible Freddie, first things first,
it must be your choice to unwind the old web.
I can only teach you how." said Mr. Cotton.

They bonded over stories of their lives in the rainforest
and realizing that they shared a common love for their
home, trust and a special friendship began to form.

15

Master Love and Compassion

"Freddie, the old web you are trapped in is simply your fears. We all have fears, so you being and feeling stuck is completely normal. Fears are actually a gift in disguise. We tend to think of them as scary things we do not wish to see, or deal with, but fears are really an opportunity to become free. You see, when you face your fears they cease to exist and that sets you free."

"It all starts with intention Freddie," continued Mr. Cotton, "Intention is your silent will. It is what you truly want the outcome of your actions to be. All actions start with an intention, the reason why you are doing something. If this intention is heartfelt and sincere, it holds a tremendous amount of power." So with the power of Freddie's purest intention to let go of his fears, guided by Mr. Cotton's wisdom, the web of fears began to unravel and release its hold over him.

They made their way to a point with a beautiful view, looking out over the rainforest. They sat in silence for a while. They watched the sun slowly descend over the horizon, disappearing into a deep pink, orange and amber glow. Quiet and still without a word or a movement, they sat. The stars and the moon lit up and sparkled in the night sky. After roughly an hour Mr. Cotton spoke,

"All you need to learn and achieve is all already within you."

As the night grew late, the new friends relaxed into a peaceful sleep.

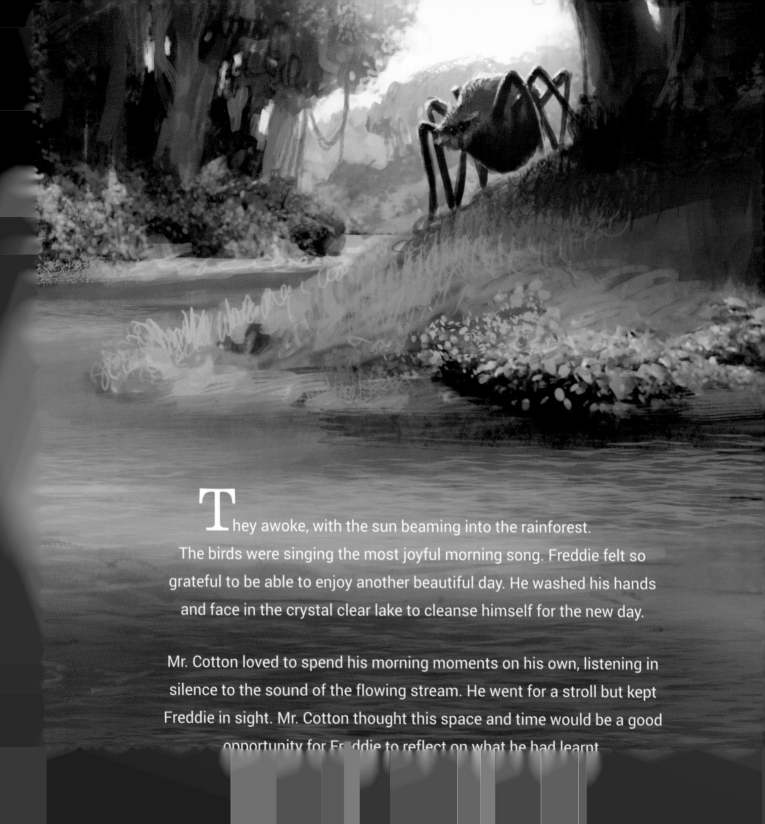

They awoke, with the sun beaming into the rainforest. The birds were singing the most joyful morning song. Freddie felt so grateful to be able to enjoy another beautiful day. He washed his hands and face in the crystal clear lake to cleanse himself for the new day.

Mr. Cotton loved to spend his morning moments on his own, listening in silence to the sound of the flowing stream. He went for a stroll but kept Freddie in sight. Mr. Cotton thought this space and time would be a good opportunity for Freddie to reflect on what he had learnt.

"*F*reddie my boy, it is time," Mr. Cotton called out.

"Time for what?" asked Freddie.

"*To begin the journey up the mountain,*" replied Mr. Cotton.

He led Freddie to the foot of a high mountain. The mountain was huge with sheer rock faces, towering high into the clouds. The lush green hillside was covered with bushes and small trees. The trees and bushes were full of wild, colorful flowers.

Together they stood at the foot of the mountain. Freddie and Mr. Cotton began to ascend the path leading up to the top of the mountain. Every so often they passed small pools with insects skipping across the water. Mr. Cotton walked at a steady pace without stopping. Freddie started to trail behind.

Mr. Cotton continued walking easily up the large steps of the path. He has surely done this many times before, Freddie thought to himself, breathing heavily. His youthful legs, although accustomed to walking a lot, began to struggle on the steep slope of the mountain. Just when Freddie thought he could not go on, the path leveled out. Mr. Cotton said,

"Right. Let us stop for a rest. I want to tell you a story."

"A magnificent lotus flower lived in the King's pond. Its soft beautiful pink petals bathed in the sun. The lotus flower took great pleasure in displaying its beauty for the King and all the King's friends to see. The lotus flower came to realize that the time had come to move on in the circle of life. So it produced a seed that fell to the bottom of the pond. The once magnificent lotus flower closed its petals, withered and fell apart to be blown away by the wind."

"The seed lay at the bottom of the pond underneath layers of thick mud. Although it was a long way away from the surface of the water, the seed's intention was to grow into a beautiful lotus flower. Still a hard young seed, the process of time in the thick mud softened the seed's shell.

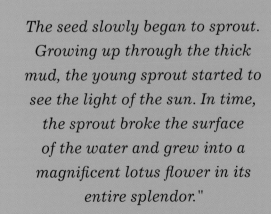

The seed slowly began to sprout. Growing up through the thick mud, the young sprout started to see the light of the sun. In time, the sprout broke the surface of the water and grew into a magnificent lotus flower in its entire splendor."

"F*reddie,*" said Mr. Cotton, *"The lotus seed is a metaphor for life. We are like the seed. It is through the thick mud or challenges in life that we learn and grow. We become softened and strengthened by these challenges. We begin to sprout, letting our true, loving nature come to the fore in our lives. Still growing through the challenge of the water, we know that the light of the world is here. We can see it. We aspire to live more and more in the light. Until finally, we blossom into a magnificent lotus flower, breaking out of the water and living fully in the light, the radiant sun beaming down on the glory of our wide spread petals for an entire kingdom to see."*

Before they continued up the mountain, Mr. Cotton
picked some fruit from the trees that provided them shade.
He handed one to Freddie and he bit into the fruit.
The sweet nectar exploded with flavor in his mouth.
Freddie had never experienced such amazing
sensations on his tongue. It was awesome.

Freddie and Mr. Cotton continued up the mountain's challenging path. Although it was not much further to the top, the slope increased drastically, making the next thirty minutes of hiking even more challenging.

"Freddie," said Mr. Cotton, *"As you approach the end of your journey to becoming a lotus flower, the path may become even more challenging. Stay focused on your goals and your dreams in order to achieve them."*

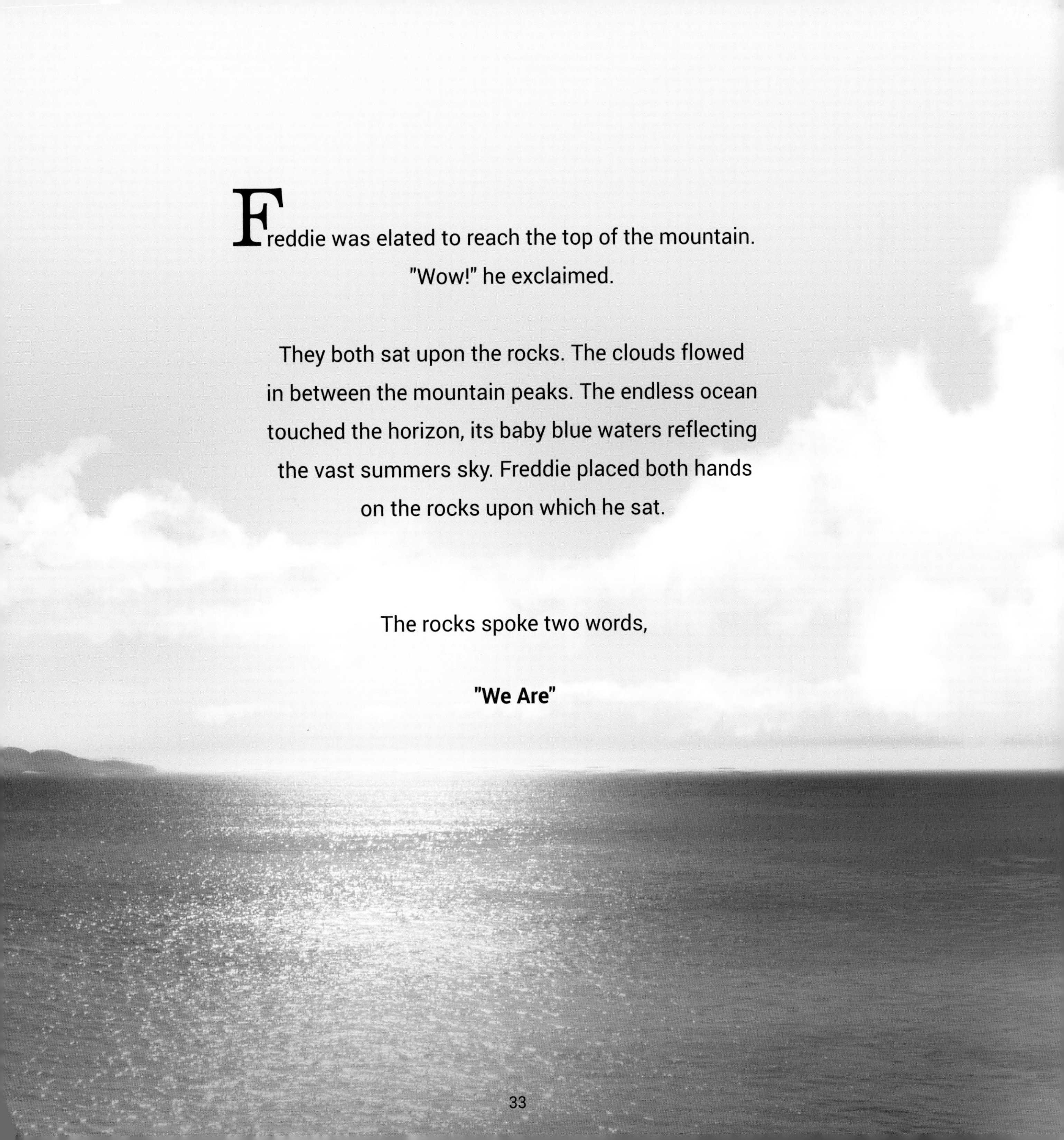

Freddie was elated to reach the top of the mountain.
"Wow!" he exclaimed.

They both sat upon the rocks. The clouds flowed
in between the mountain peaks. The endless ocean
touched the horizon, its baby blue waters reflecting
the vast summers sky. Freddie placed both hands
on the rocks upon which he sat.

The rocks spoke two words,

"We Are"

Freddie was amazed that the rocks could speak. He did not fully understand what the rocks meant in saying We are. He looked to Mr. Cotton. "Please explain the meaning, of what the rocks said."

"We are," Mr. Cotton said, "Is the truth of the universe. All things that exist are one.
The only truth about us is our very being. That we exist is that truth. Not our labels.
Not our names or titles or the things that we do. We are all beings of Light and this is the
truth of We Are. We are all equal. We are all equally special and beautiful. When you come to
know and understand this truth Freddie you will see the Light, Beauty and Joy in all things
of the world. Upon these values you can start to dream and build a new web for yourself.
A web that is light, strong and glows with brilliance, the web of your dreams."

Their journey home was long but felt as if it went quickly as Freddie pondered over all the things he had learnt from Mr. Cotton.

M r. Cotton tucked Freddie up in his bed in the middle of the magical rainforest. Before leaving he said,

"Freddie, never stop dreaming. It is important to know that by helping others realize their dreams you get closer to your own. You have been given many gifts. Share what you have learnt on your journey."

Freddie lay comfortable and filled with joy. He closed his eyes
and in his mind, he flew up through the clouds and into the stars.
He began to dream. He dreamt and a new web began to form.
It sparkled amongst the stars.

About the Author

Brent Feinberg is a best-selling children's book author. He was born in 1990 in South Africa and is an integrative healer and practitioner in consciousness based health care. Brent is passionate about empowering children and youth in order for them to live healthy fulfilled lives. He is a gentle soul who is driven to make a positive change in the world.

Other Titles include:

Freeing Freddie the Dream Weaver
The Ultimate Activity Book

Freeing Freddie the Dream Weaver
A Guide to Realizing your Dreams A Workbook

About the Illustrator

Daniel Clarke is a South African artist and animator. He was born in Cape Town and is self-taught in many mediums, including animation, painting, and production design.

freeingfreddie

Freeing Freddie

www.withlovefromfreddie.com

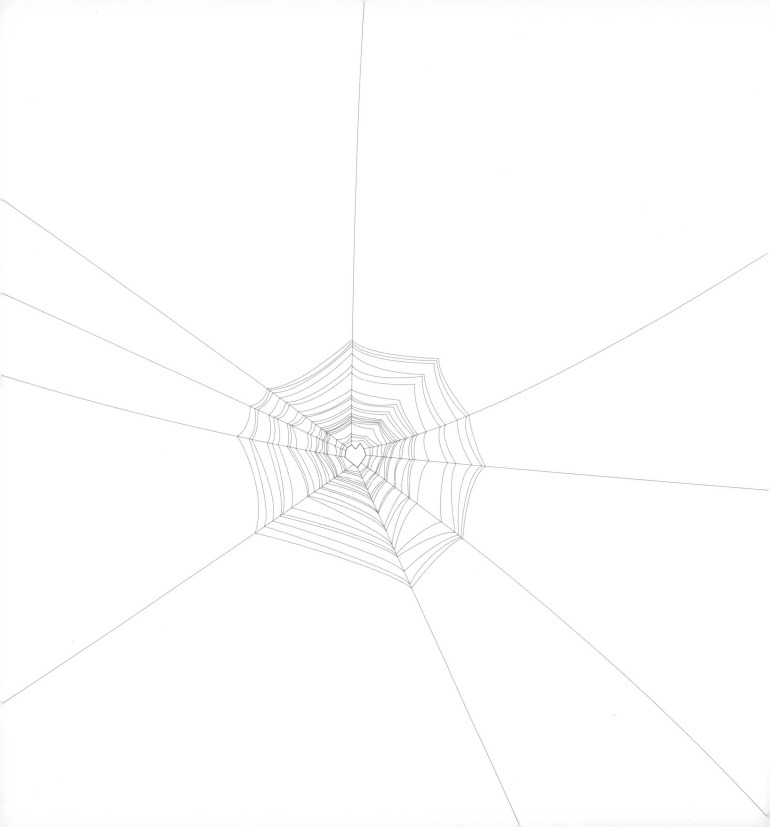

With love from FREDDIE

A portion of the profits will go towards children's education
in the United States and South Africa.

The Freeing Freddie package includes books and other products designed to enhance the conscious development of children, youth, and adults in a fun manner so that they can realize their potential. Created as a catalyst for positive social change, our products help readers discover who they are through life lessons presented through stories, activities, and workshops. The interactions build a constructive experience that enable young people to become happy, skilled individuals who will positively interact with their environment.

Our books help individuals gain insight into their own lives, their fears and dreams, and their sensitivities and challenges while enjoying a magical experience. They are filled with simple methods of self-inquiry, bringing joy to all those who read the stories and work with the activity and workbooks. These products have successfully taught people to deal with fear that can later manifest itself as anger, hate, and violence. They effectively address young people who struggle with a challenging world and need positive answers.

Everyone who has read and worked with our books has been influenced in a positive way. Young people have been inspired to look beyond their current circumstance, to dream, and to imagine a brighter future—a world that they are now empowered to create. Adults have learned to look within themselves and determine whether they are operating from a place of negativity and fear that is adversely affecting their own lives and well as those of their loved ones. The workbook provides tools that enable readers to make needed change.

When a child and adult read our books together, the entire family is positively affected. Here is a family of products that allow people to gain greater understanding of one another and learn to bridge the gap between parent and child.

THE FREEING FREDDIE SERIES

Freeing Freddie the Dream Weaver— Ultimate Activity Book ♥

Freeing Freddie the Dream Weaver—Ultimate Activity Book is a fun-filled book with activities for children of all ages. Practical tools help children deal with their fears and guide them in building magical dreams. Children will be delighted by simple recipes, puzzles, games, and a variety of kid-friendly crafts. Included are stickers as well as beautiful illustrations waiting to be colored. This book can be used alone or along with the *Freeing Freddie the Dream Weaver* picture book.

$16.95 US / $25.95 CAN
56 pages including 4 sticker pages
9.75 x 9.75-inch paperback
Children's Activity Book
ISBN 978-0-7570-0459-9 (PB) / ISBN 978-0-7570-5459-4 (EB)

Freeing Freddie the Dream Weaver A Guide to Realizing Your Dreams— A Workbook ♥

This special workbook—which can be used alone or alongside the *Freeing Freddie the Dream Weaver* picture book—guides children in letting go of their fears and empowers them to create their own magical dreams. The exercises are practical and easy to do, but most important, they are fun, insightful, and filled with joy. A dynamic tool, this workbook includes visualizations that children can download from a website and listen to at their leisure. Each visualization takes children on a journey of self-discovery, enabling them to escape from a place of fear and find love, compassion, and success.

$19.95 US / $29.95 CAN
72 pages
9.75 x 9.75-inch paperback
Workbook
ISBN 978-0-7570-0460-5 (PB) / ISBN 978-0-7570-5460-0 (EB)

For more information about our books,
visit our website at www.squareonepublishers.com